Sacred Scoop

Feel the magic in the moments

Kamalika Bhattacharya

Ukiyoto Publishing

Dedication

I frequently get choked up when I think about the misery that individuals endure. I appreciate everyone who helped me depict my poems and concepts.

I would like to express my gratitude to my family for continuing to support me as I complete my task. Mom, I appreciate how you always smooth out the edges of my imperfections. I appreciate you encouraging me to persevere no matter what. Although I mourn you, Dad, I still draw inspiration from you in all my writing. Thanks to my "best friends" for lending me a healing hand filled with love and care. My favourite place to vent, rest, recharge, and re-energize my spirit.

They are all beloved people, without whom I couldn't have created such layers of emotions. Finally, my mentor, Mike who guided me to turn the emotions into words in the most unflinching manner. And thanks to the person whom I call my home.

Contents

She

She dwelled in the world full of pain,ā

And never charted down her gain,

Her dreams were undefined and unlimited,

And lit up her way.

Also enriched her day.

She often thinks what, she could impart,

To heal her broken heart.

Those cotton clouds and that wash blue sky,

At times, rips her soul apart.

The warrior in her, battles all the odds,

But the small little things , some times look flawed.

Her beauty , Her innocence

Her war goddess self, blinded by her own reflect.

She is a guarded woaman,

Who never lets you in,

Her battle cries are not less than roars,

And she swallows her pride within.

She denies to be the one ,

Who could be fixed.

She is equivalent to a sharp weapon,

Watchful of all the risks.

She keeps her faith,

Through all the hardships she sails,
Her prayers protect her and never
Let her fail.

Cheerful eyes, entails grace,
Her generosity and poise,
Neither seeking praise, nor power at all,
She garners her blessings
And stands tall.

She has her hopes, and swears by her dreams,
She is a powerhouse deep within,
All she wants is the right anchor,
Who will call her queen and
Be her king.

Quiet Admiration

I admire you,
For who you are and there are millions of reasons apart,
I find light in your gaze
That often lifts my heart.

When I count the stars at night,
I admire that wonderful sight,
I may not express how much I adore you,
But your thought makes my face bright.

I may not hold you in my arms every day,
But the winds silent touch would do,
I may not rest my head on you,
But your words I carry through.
You are not less than a miracle,
And my reason to smile,
The thought of us electrifies the urge,
And makes it worthwhile.
I won't ever deny the charm of your attraction,
For you are my heartthrob never allows the retraction.

A wish to fill your heart, is something I often desire,
for you are the only one who could set my heart ablaze.

I see you in my sunrise, in the reflection of light and water,

Which I pleasingly gaze.

Be it dusk or dawn your face surfaces as my innate desire.

As I surrender to the love alter, I take your name,

I will never utter it again, and always hide my flame.

Your touch took me away through bliss, beauty, and pain,

For this is my way of admiration, it is deep and difficult to explain.

Your thought is my strength and is an endless passion.

Let it burn quietly but never disdain.

A Moment of Love

A day filled with your thoughts,
Always keeps me going,
You're in my dreams,
that goes without saying.

Your smile brightens up my day,
On your lap I wish I could lay,
after a tiresome day,
Looking at you brings me joy,
Everything that smells like you,
Often makes me feel coy.

Being a loner, I had my setbacks,
Being an admirer, I hold myself back.
You are the one who rules my heart,
And it causes exponential pain to stay apart.

I will never be able to tell you,
That you're precious to me,
For my feelings are true and
Will remain alike for you.
My prayers were answered,
The day we met. As a dream cease to be.

I thank the almighty everyday,
For bestowing a precious gift to me.

You brighten up my world,
with the rays of a star,
No matter where you are,
You're gentle, you are true.
You are beyond compare,
And my heart adores you.

Rose

The rose speaks of love,
amidst the cluster of thorns,
Each petal beautiful and soft,
Represents the beauty
Of soulful love.

With fragrance deep, and love to keep,
Memories to cherish and goes on repeat.
My words for you are meant to be true,
Darling heart!! I love you.

In love, in anger its true,
a single piece has million clues,
a flower that is loved by all,
when assimilates like a priceless pearl.

A rose has the stillness, and depth of an ocean,
When given with love, turns to be a jewel.
The beauty it holds pierces the heart,
 In the vine it flourishes like a piece of an art.

My single red rose,

With love it grows, sprinkled with love,

Never fails to impress and always glows.

The red ones whispers passion,

The pink one oozes love,

Yellow shines bright and pretty,

Brighter than the morning sun.

So, is the bunch of white,

Looks life a fairy tale and

 Reflects enchanting light.

Red one blooms in winter,

And add colours to the season,

Each day with a grace,

As each petal unfolds

And awakens a supreme passion.

Long live that bright red rose,

Which brings millions of heart so close.

When it slides into the book,

 Memories blends along and froze.

Reverie

Dreams give us a goal,
The one we want to pursue,
And wish they may come true,
Dreams are something we live for,
While we long to make it better and flew.

The darkest night, often steal away our hope,
And leave us to weep, Dreams are tender,
Wonder if they are dreams,
I've ever had one worth it,
For the starlit sky upon us,
Gives me a hope, that your love for me is so deep and
We have millions of scope.

When you hold me tight,
In the dreams, your passion fills my heart,
And my mind screams of thousand fantasies,
With you living thousand miles apart.
I wont ever give up on you,
For you are my ultimate knight,
My life revolves around you,
And with you everything feels allright.

I wish I could tame the time,

To treasure you in my heart,

Precious moments with you are unique,

And always will remain class apart.

Weaving myriad fantasies,

And thousands of thoughts,

My senses are hypnotised with that charming smile

And those bright twinkling eyes,

I wish your fingers swipe off my face,

Giving it a gentle caress,

I reminisce your naughty whispers as I lay awake

Dreams are often magical,

So be it, I wish your hand in mine,

As I put off to sleep.

Isolation

A hand to hold,
A consoling embrace,
and love unknown,
full of grace.

A pain runs through my vein,
And heart too aches, I long for you in silence
and that drives me insane.

Each day comes with a challenge,
Every night I mourn, I never confess,
But, I am tired of facing the world alone.
My soul is withdrawn,
I am not scared of loneliness,
I fear of losing you,
In this world full of madness.

Thinking of all this, my heart often aches,
And chills run down my spine, a silence creep in
And my soul refuse to rise and shine.
Trapped with uncertain things,
Hell, breaks on my heels,
I gasp for air at times,

As if I fail to breathe.
I continue to soar alone,
Till the end of time,
My demons are kept away,
 to let me whine and shine.

I try to chase you every time,
But you're miles away,
That pristine feel of touching you,
Has not yet melted away.

You're the only spark, left in my dark world,
That brings me a smile, waiting for you is painful,
Yet I seek for a warmer time.
I need you, like a heart needs a beat,
You're my pink petals and my redden dreams.

I don't know what's written in fate,
To soften my fall and ease my escape
As the tear drip on my wrist
Reminds me my loneliness
and your strong embrace.

Sacred Touch

The sweetest smile, that echoes your own,
Velvet touch that my heart has ever known.
Two different souls, blended so well,
Seamless it looks, when their patterns interweave.

Our eyes filled with, love for each other,
Profess what we feel, I can't get over the sound,

When I hear my name on your lips.
When my heart undergoes turmoil,
and the walls close on to me,
 Your gentle voice replenishes my soul,
And brings tranquillity upon me.
When I look deep in your eyes,
And that warm smile on your face,
My hands raise to prayer,
And I know that there is no better place.

Against the odds with unending spirit,
A diffused passion and care,
Every moment is eventful and true,
I count my blessings twice,
While thinking of you.

We are not perfect, neither ought to be,
Amidst these voices and whispers,
Your arms are the only place,
I ever wanted to be.
You're my sunshine,
All the way long,
My heart is restless yet to you it belong.

Sweet Innuendo

Your optimism inspires me, your courage entices me,

Your warmth comforts me, you mean so much to me.

Whenever I feel low, you come as a respite,

Your humour wallows my worries

Your love often communicates to my soul.

Your care rejuvenates me,

More and always more.

With your helping hands,

I find reasons to share, you make me feel secure,

By always being there.

I admire you for gauging my needs,

With such minute details,

You are my core strength,

Out of the fairytale.

I thank my stars for this and more,

Unknown is what that luck restores.

Anxiety, trouble and a whole lot of woe,

There are innumberable things that remains difficult without you.

A caring heart will always be near,

Amidst the care and beautiful cheer,

Thoughts of being wanderlust and wanting to roam,

You embrace my difficulties and take away my fear.
With you the comfort is endless and
Feels like I am home.

You're my voyage,
My restless shore,
Life won't be perfect, nor it has been before.
When storms are raging and nights turn long,
I'll just be there always along.

Entrusted

Love can't be defined in a word or two,
An undying bond that keeps us glued,
When loneliness obscures the sky,
Our memories keep me high.

The gentle touch and that smiling face,
Those caring words and your warm embrace,
Your memories are there all over the place,
All the corners here and that parched terrace.

Our passion has kept it ignited across the miles,
Our love has come a long way,
Withstanding the test of time,
There is no other place
I want to be.
Your heart is my home,
and always will be.

There is always a person,
Who feels like the biggest star,
He feels so close, even when he is far.
He makes me complete
I trust him so much.
He is my hero and my compass.

His love cannot be measured,
And his heartfelt touch.
His kindness and love are immense and true.
I entrusted him my body and soul,
Because he can make my grey sky turn blue.

Without him the walls will close on me,
Love is my everything,
In ways big and small,
I haven't told him yet,
He's the best thing ever
I have experienced so far.
He turns my world bold,
He's precious than gold.

There are days when am scattered,
Wish he could be with me for a while,
As my eyes sparkle to
See that sweet and charming smile
It fills me with pleasure
When he holds me close,
A pocketful of sunshine
He's uniquely different
Who I never wish to lose.
All I need him to know is,
There is no end of desires and more,

All I know deep down in true,

You're my forever

And I love you.

Cold Night

A quiet cold night,
Silent and rare
I just woke up and
 couldn't find you near.

The days became long,
And nights were cold.
Well, age is just numbers
we never get old.

I miss your touch,
Your tender love for me,
Those smirks of your eyes,
And that candid smile
Matted with your glee
Being with you is all I want
But I miss the touch of your hand.

Watching the crimson hues of the dusk,
I saw the sun melting away
As I dream of the past, sweet memories comfort me
And holds a promise to last.

I miss the way; you held me close
And the beat of your heart,
Days and night,
I think of you even when we are miles apart.

When the night takes over,
And the stars light up the dark.
I miss you by my side and wish often for a dreamy ride.

Veneration

Before you adore her face,
uplift her spirits with love and grace,
Treat her with love and respect.

Loving each other deeply
 is one of the greatest wealth,
respect and understanding
entangled with love
impacts our mind and health.

Always admire the excitement,
And adore the calm.
Trust is the greatest gift,
and it never allows to harm.

Joy and grief are unputdownable,
And marks the course of life,
Learn to sail through the toughest storms
To learn the skills of the ride.
A lesson learnt through experience
Is always a blessing and cure,
That makes you prepare

For the things you are unsure.

Love must set us free,
When its laced with friendship and glee,
Keeping harmony eases our boundaries,
That evokes respects
Quite unknowingly.
To take the path of progress,
Tolerance is the key,
Love is bigger than war,
It is denoted in the history.
So, love more, not less,
With respect redefined,
When it encompasses
And touches life with
Striking positiveness.
It brings more shine and
Causes enlightenment.

Love and respect should never fall apart,
Because we live once, blessed are those souls,
Who have braced love and never missed the chance.
Hating someone will take away all the positive vibes,
Wear the smile and let them wonder
The reason as you while.

Away

It hurts me though
But it feels so good as well,
To love you more and
 endure the pain which brings me to hell.
 I wish you could see the pain,
Caused by the distance between us,
I have given up on many things
For the only person I trust.

I trust you in the darkest hours,
I believe in your words,
Even when things get complicated,
I look beyond to gain rewards.
My instinct gives me strength,
To hold on to you,
No matter what I know,
Somewhere deeper and
Somewhat like you.

Sometimes I want it simple,
I want you by me,
While looking in your eyes,
I wish to set my soul free.

Your thoughts keep me awake through night,
Loving you feels so right,
Hoping you will feel the same,
If not more, but little insane.
Love can't be measured; I know it very well.
Feelings are precious, and words will always fail.
Treasure the blessing that you have,
Only with the right person who
Responds to your unspoken words.
 It's not for the weak, or those who're scared of pain,
It's for the ignited hearts, those who cry only
While walking across the rains.

The hope to see each other, every now and then
When each minute you feel, the urge to hear
Him again.
Distance can't be counted by miles between the two,
Its about surviving the moments that prepares you
It strengthens the heart and enriches the soul,
Because, when the love is true, you learn to fight
All your fears,
 even though your eyes are welled up and
moist with tears.

Bespoken

Those intense eyes could stir my soul,
As a glory glanced down
I dream, I falter and rose,
I got hooked to that look,
Like a fantasy turning into a dream
Deeper they were pulling me in.

Those unspoken words
Hidden in your eyes,
Intense they look
After making me rise,
The twinkle in them
transports me to heaven
those charming pair
had the zeal to shine
he is my pride
and unapologetically mine.

Sometimes I wonder
What is it that I could not see
Perhaps his innocent quests
And his deepest love for me.
He knows to speak without a touch

It fills my heart with pride
And caress it so much.
The spark lits me up
And linked me to my heart and soul.
Searching for true love
Glowing and vibrant
Those filled with magical essence
And a powerful goal.

Consumed by desire and pain,
Charged by infinite zeal,
Burning with fierce love
And smeared by thoughtful heal.
All these and much more
Lifts my soul above,
Manifesting peace and bliss
With everlasting love.

Let those eyes always bespoke,
Of what is yet to unleash.
For eyes have a language
Of its own and the eyes
Often show the strength of your soul.

Rain and Pain

A beautiful mountain plain,

Green lush and gorgeous terrain,

As the clouds melt

I pour out my weight,

The weight of all my pain

That catches up with the rain.

A disguised brain, soaked in love and

Immersed in pain.

Those unending summer that promises

to stay longer, they are induced with enormous emotions,

and a handful of pleasant notions.

Some are even more gorgeous

Displays outrageous passion.

The summer, that brews the adverse

And nurture a storm.

Also, longs for that cold breeze

That only rain brings along.

Forests and fields get to life, only when it rains,

Although thunder brings fear and the feeling of disdain.

The wet and cold streets, washed and shine bright

Absorbs the warmth of you. That light drizzle young
At heart is drenched, in love and melt like dew.
The heartaches, in the bed of tears
When the love is deep and nurtured for years.

Moon Light

Just thinking of you,
The moments of those darkest nights.
Cool breeze caressing my hair
And whispering in my ears that we are yet
To witness the brightest light.

In the mysterious chambers of night,
Hiding behind those clouds,
It walks across the aisle,
As an empress of the night.
It denies to come out of the veil
And spread the pageantry of light.

Watching the silver moonbeam,
His heart beating against mine,
Interlocking with eachother
We realize our soul collides,
I could sense the rule of your desires against mine,
And that add sparkles to my eyes,
I want you to stay inclined,
A pocketful of heavenly bliss
Untouched and yet destined.

All these delights and that gentle breeze,

when steps inside to peep,

covering me with a velvet rug,

I say to myself no more illusions

Let the night gaze,

As I am drawn to close my eyes

Capturing the soothing moonlight.

Silence

Silence is powerful
The sound and syllabus are
Unique to express.
But yet the unspoken
Has infinite grace.

At times of grief and sorrow,
Silence is crucial and felt
It pierces our soul but often
Heals our heart and helps it melt.

A millions of desires and unfathomable guilt,
Not bigger than any sorrow over which it's been built.
At night, we feel the stillness
And amidst that silence sways,
The nature has its sound and score,
Out of the staggered ways.

Silence is not only meant for
Broken hearts, also beckons the thinking souls,
Who simply loves to keep things apart,
Clouds that gather to bring them together
Knows those boundaries and dreams,
They are meaningful and poignant
For it has a power within.

Optimistic

Having trust that every dark night
Will come to an end.
A ray of hope carries optimism.
 Out of those endless tasks and to do list,
Sort out that ignites your spirit.
Chasing a dream that
Makes you strong
 Is worth a fight,
Disapprove the challenges
 That creeps in
And you'll definitely see a light.

Overcome your fears
And doubts from this epiphany of world.
Rebuild your soul and by shedding
Your team alone and turn cold.
You've to be resilient and fierce,
If you wish to win, a fearless heart,
And an unapologetic spirit will never be dim.

Hold on to your dreams,

Turn them to your passion,

Let the fine within you guide your emotions.

Take change of your happiness.

Because it begins with you,

And rise like a wild fire

And see the life renew.

Renewed Love

My heart is quiet,
Must have seen you,
My heart is bruised
 And love renewed.
Broken inside, but
I have faith in that
For love is enormous,
Even when it drifts apart.

It's not deal, the words can do magic
And proportionately heal.
It removes the creases
Of my frown
And lift's my bewitching soul.
Bringing in peace
And not letting me down.
Those scars that you gifted me,
Are yet to heal,
For you they were perhaps no big deal,
I smile at them now,
Because they help me to look beyond.
That never stopped me to love you
And made me strong.

I have chosen to hum a new love song

Where in respect comes along.

For love is different,

It does not demand empathy,

It is given out of love

That is no sympathy.

Commitment

An eternal commitment,
Which is more than an emotion
Is ought to last, because love slowly creeps in
Before you know it.
It expands and spell the cast.

And with deep desires buried,
Inside with a sigh I ask
Promise me your heart,
Until the slip of time.

Smile when you think of us,
Get reminded of the hugs.
That makes you feel safe,
Not the big occasions,
Promise me those
Small moments of laughter
Amidst the chaotic life.

Our heart and soul knotted
With each other would be
The moment I cherish the most,
No matter if that has been
Captured by a photograph to tag and post.

Your illuminating smile is my biggest gem,
No matter whether I am with you,
Yesterday, tomorrow, and today.
It is and it will always be you.

Empowered

Time and People knocked me down,
 Knowingly unknowingly they tore me apart.
With words, with actions they tarnished my soul,
But my spirit survived it all
And I refused to give up.
That is empowerment.

Emotions wallow you,
You learn to emerge out of the pain
Those tough moments where feel numb,
Life looks meaningless.

It hurts like hell and you
Tell yourself it is not easy
But I will not let myself
Shatter like this.
That is empowerment.

Broken heart and life plunge you down
As emotion drains down.
It is like a plague.
The person you love
Will always make things easier for you,

Not break you.
To have the power;
learn to ignore the mess.
Be with one who heals you
Not add to your battles.
Broken is also beautiful.
That is empowerment.

Sculpted

Is she fixed like a portrait,
They call her a woman,
Who is ought to be picture perfect.
At times like a daughter and
Sometimes like a spouse.
She possesses the power to
Fix that is scattered and louse.

Her lips like a rose,
Humming her favourite tune.
Those sculpted cheekbones,
Reminds of the hot sand dunes.

Adoring the colour bright,
She enchanted in.
Some fiddle to hear,
And to lift her chin...

She has everything, yet nothing.
She mourns during pale noons,
When even the shadow darkens,
Stable, patient, waiting
Standing at one spot as

A lady of the night,
Waiting eagerly perhaps
For her shining armour,
May be her knight.

A timid ray of love
Beaming across her face
A stolen simple look,
Bound to ascend.

When she steps down to Love,
Evening came crashing,
The saffron waves floating
Across the sky,
Her fondness fading
And passion melting
From the corner of her eyes.

Her face radiates grace,
Her joy fills her days
As she's full of kindness
Angels guide her ways.

Those eyes that is filled with sunshine bright,
Like heaven's miracle and charming divine.
Gentleness is just a part her rebel nature often outshines.

She's a woman who believes to stand upright.

Live, Love, Respect.

As she is the best version of being Sculpted.

About the Author

Kamalika Bhattacharya

Kamalika Bhattacharya has written poems, short stories, and editorials for a variety of publications. Her work skillfully blends passion, drama, and love.

She earned degrees in mass communication and print journalism from IIMC. She has years of valuable professional experience working for various print and media companies. Her desire to travel drives her to write down her thoughts and create a variety of storylines. She accurately measures the components that make the story last because she is an avid reader and observer. She works hard to convey the range of emotions that exist in human life by providing the characters with appropriate intonations. She writes with passion and a wide range of strong emotions. Her previous solo book, Smitten by

Love, a collection of short stories, is just one instance.